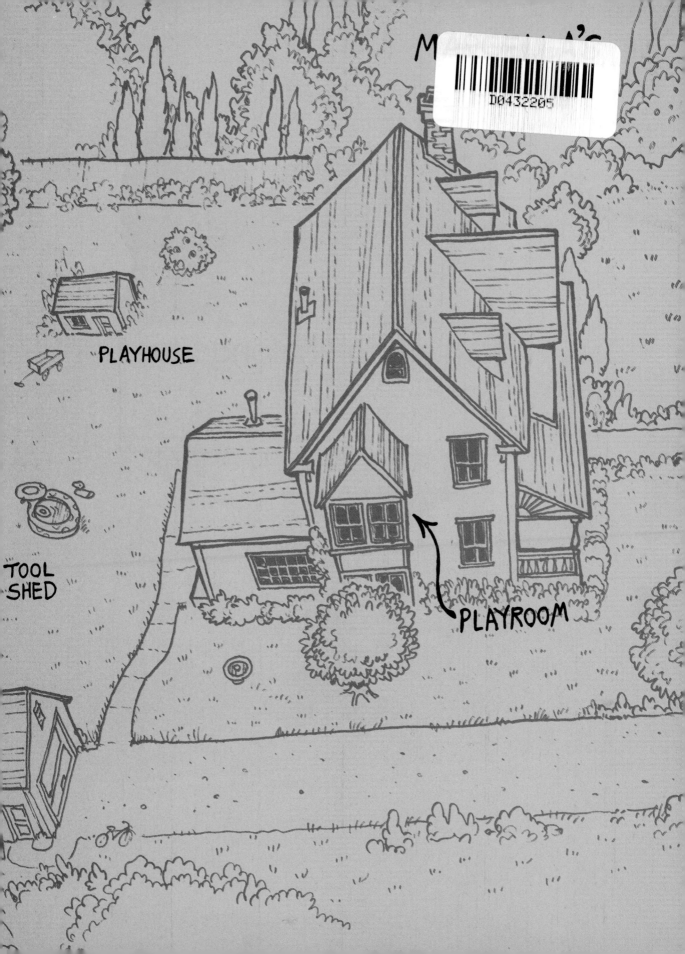

This book belongs to:

Fay

Raggedy Ann & Andy's

GROW
AND
LEARN
LIBRARY

VOLUME 6

BABETTE'S SCARY NIGHT

A LYNX BOOK

This book is published by Lynx Books, a division of Lynx Communications, Inc., 41 Madison Avenue, New York, New York 10010. The name "Lynx" together with the logotype consisting of a stylized head of a lynx is a trademark of Lynx Communications, Inc.

Raggedy Ann and Andy's Grow-and-Learn Library, the names and depictions of Raggedy Ann, Raggedy Andy and all related characters are trademarks of Macmillan, Inc.

Marcella waved good-bye to her dolls in the playroom.
She and her parents were going somewhere very special.
They were going camping in the woods for the weekend.
Marcella had told Raggedy Ann all about the other
camping trips she had taken.

"Camping in the woods is lots of fun," Raggedy Ann told the dolls. "Marcella said that you get to sleep outside in a tent in a nice soft sleeping bag under the moon and the stars."

"Wow!" said Raggedy Andy. "That does sound like fun!"

"I wish *we* were going camping," said Tim the Toy Soldier.

"I'm glad we're not," Babette the French Doll began to say. "It's dark in the woods at night and . . ."

Before Babette had a chance to explain exactly how she felt about camping outside, Raggedy Andy interrupted her. "Hey, I just thought of a great plan!" he shouted excitedly. "While Marcella is away, we can go on a camping trip of our own."

"How?" asked Sunny Bunny, hopping up and down.

"What would we use for a tent?" asked Tim the Toy Soldier.

"And sleeping bags?" added Greta the Dutch Doll.

"What would we do for a light?" asked Babette in a very small voice, which nobody heard.

Then The Camel with the Wrinkled Knees spoke up. "I've never been camping before," he said slowly. "But maybe we could pretend the playhouse is our tent."

"Why, Camel, what a good idea," agreed Raggedy Andy. "And we can use our blankets as sleeping bags," he added.

And that's just what they did. All the dolls packed up their blankets and pillows as fast as they could and trooped outside to the playhouse.

All the dolls except Babette, that is. Babette didn't want to camp outside. She was very happy in the playroom—especially since the playroom had a little light that stayed on all night long. Babette knew that *outside* was sure to be very, very dark—and she didn't like that idea at all.

"Come on, Babette!" Raggedy Ann called. "We'd better try to get everything set up while it's still light out!"

Babette didn't know what to do. She didn't want to go. But she also didn't want the other dolls to know she was *afraid* of the dark.

Then Raggedy Ann called her again.

Very, very slowly, Babette picked up her blanket and headed for the playhouse.

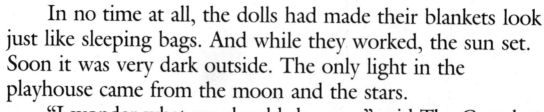

In no time at all, the dolls had made their blankets look just like sleeping bags. And while they worked, the sun set. Soon it was very dark outside. The only light in the playhouse came from the moon and the stars.

"I wonder what we should do now," said The Camel with the Wrinkled Knees.

"Marcella said that she and her parents tell stories," Raggedy Ann told them. "She said her favorite stories are the kind that one person starts, and then someone else tells the next part, and then someone else . . ."

"What a great idea!" interrupted Sunny Bunny. "May I go first?" he asked. "I know the beginning of a story I think everyone will like."

So Sunny Bunny began.

"Once upon a time in a faraway land, there lived an evil wizard who ruled over a place called the Enchanted Forest. It was called 'enchanted' because the evil wizard had put all the animals who lived in the forest under a spell."

"I know what kind of spell he put on the animals," said Raggedy Andy. But before he could tell, Babette let out a gasp.

"Look! Out there—it's the wizard. He's coming to put a spell on *us!*" Babette shouted.

At once the dolls rushed over to the playhouse window.

"There's no wizard out there, Babette," said Raggedy Andy.

"It's just a shadow from those trees," Raggedy Ann assured her.

"Besides," added Sunny Bunny, "the wizard in *our* story never leaves the Enchanted Forest."

They all sat back down, and Raggedy Andy continued.

"The evil wizard cast a spell on the animals in the forest that made them do anything he asked. Then he ordered them to sneak up to the homes of the people who lived in the forest and play tricks on the children who were sleeping."

All of the dolls laughed at Raggedy Andy's story. Even Babette laughed—until she heard a scratching noise at the door.

"It's the animals—they're here!" Babette shouted. "They've come to play tricks on us!" She buried her face in Raggedy Ann's soft back.

All of the dolls looked a little frightened. Everyone had heard the scratching noise.

"I'm sure that noise is not from enchanted animals," said Raggedy Ann with a little smile. "Why don't we just go and see what it is?"

So Raggedy Ann and Raggedy Andy walked over and opened the playhouse door.

In scampered Raggedy Dog and Raggedy Cat.
"So here you are," Raggedy Dog said. Raggedy Dog and Raggedy Cat had gone running around the house when Marcella left. When they got back to the playroom, they discovered that everyone was gone.

"We were looking all over for you," Raggedy Cat said to the others.

The Camel with the Wrinkled Knees told them about going camping and how Raggedy Andy was telling a special story. Then Tim and Percy the Policeman Doll pushed their blankets together to make room for Raggedy Dog and Raggedy Cat.

Bubbles the Clown thought of the first trick the enchanted animals played on the children.

"One night," Bubbles began, "the animals crept quietly into the children's playrooms when they were fast asleep. Then they took all of their toys and dolls and blocks and threw them all over the floor. What a mess!"

The other dolls thought this was a very mean trick.

CRASH! Before Bubbles could tell them what happened next, something fell to the floor with a bang.

"The animals have come to mess up the playhouse!" gasped Babette.

Greta laughed. "I don't think so, Babette. I just knocked over this little chair."

Bubbles continued. "Well, the children were very upset when they saw what the animals had done. Since they were very good children, they spent all day putting everything back where it belonged. When the wizard heard this, he became so angry that he sent the animals to play another trick on them.

"This time he told the animals to crawl into every closet and every drawer and mess up all of the children's clothes. Then the children would get in trouble with their mothers and fathers."

"That trick didn't work either," said The Camel with the Wrinkled Knees. "Because the children saw the mess and put everything away before their parents even woke up.

"By now, the children were getting pretty tired of these tricks, though. So they all got together and came up with a plan."

"They decided to wait up and catch whoever was playing these tricks on them!" said Raggedy Dog.

"Oh, no!" the dolls gasped, delighted with this brave plan. All the dolls except for Babette. Babette didn't think it was a very good idea to wait up for the animals.

"But it would be very dark in the middle of the night," she whispered.

Again, Babette spoke in such a little voice, the other dolls didn't even hear her.

"That night," continued Raggedy Dog, "the children sat up in their beds until they heard a lot of scraping and scratching and other noises that animals make. And then the children poured out of their homes and surprised them."

"Instead of playing another trick on the children," Raggedy Ann said, "the animals stopped right where they were. When they realized that the children weren't afraid of them, the wizard's spell was broken.

"You see," Raggedy Ann continued, looking right at Babette, "the wizard's magic only worked when the children were afraid."

"Did the animals ever come back?" Babette asked.

"Oh yes," answered Raggedy Ann. "They came back to play with the children. The animals always wished they could tell the children that it was the wizard's spell that made them play the tricks, but they couldn't. So they decided that they would be good friends to the children instead, and this helped make up for the trouble they had caused."

"THE END!" said Babette happily. Babette had enjoyed the story after all.

Then all of the dolls were about to settle down for the night when they heard "Whooooooooo, whooooooooooo," from somewhere outside.

"I wonder what that is," said Raggedy Andy.

"I'll go look," Babette said as she walked to the window.

"It's just an old hoot owl," she told them with a laugh. "There's nothing out there to be afraid of."

So the tired dolls climbed back in their blankets and tucked themselves in for the night.

"I'm proud of you, Babette," Raggedy Ann whispered very softly.

But Babette didn't answer. She had fallen fast asleep.

RAGGEDY
LAND

HOLE
IN
FENCE

DEEP
DEEP
WOODS